This igloo book belongs to:

....

igloobooks

Published in 2018
by Igloo Books Ltd
Cottage Farm
Sywell
NN6 0BJ
www.igloobooks.com

STA002 0318
8 10 11 9 7
ISBN 978-1-78343-586-9

Illustrated by Ian Cunliffe

Printed and manufactured in China

IAN CUNLIFFE

Megaboy

igloobooks

SOMEWHERE IN A QUIET GARDEN...

A boy called Alfie is playing with his dog, Raff.
He seems like a normal boy.

The superheroes study maps, draw plans and watch over the town. There's just one thing standing in their way...

Dastardly Dad marches the scruffy pair to the
bathroom and plops them in the soapy water.

LATER THAT DAY...

Superheroes need super-food, so Megaboy mixes up a **super-powered** bowl of spaghetti, sweets and ice cream.

Megaboy and Megadog whizz towards the front door, ready to save the town again. Dastardly Dad stops them and orders them to clean their room.

Megaboy trudges up the stairs, grumbling.

The pair zip-line down to the tree house.

As the sun begins to set, the duo plan, scheme and plot a way to stop Dastardly Dad.

TIE

TRAP

SLAP

BYE!

"I've got it!" shouts Megaboy, jumping and tumbling across the tree house.

Suddenly, there's a huge

THUNK!

"Uh-oh," says Megaboy, sheepishly.

They peek out the tree house and see the fallen ladder.

Suddenly, the back door swings open...

Dastardly Dad helps
Megaboy and Megadog
climb down the ladder.
He's saved them!

"It's time for bed,"
says Dastardly Dad.
"I'll bring you both a big
mug of hot chocolate
to warm you up."

THAT NIGHT...

Megaboy and Megadog decide that Dastardly Dad isn't so bad after all. Dastardly Dad tucks the pair up in bed and reads them a bedtime story.

Thanks for saving us, MEGADAD!

From now on, the superhero trio decide that, instead of battling each other, they would work together to keep the town, or sometimes each other, safe!